Disney · PIXAR

TOY STORY 4

AUTUMN PUBLISHING

There was once a little boy called Andy, and he had a favourite toy called Woody. Woody was a pull-string cowboy and he looked after all of Andy's toys, helping with any problems they had.

One of Woody's best friends was a doll called Bo Peep. They would often work together to help the other toys.

One stormy night, Woody was outside Andy's house after rescuing a toy. He gasped when he looked through the window. He saw Andy's mum place Bo and her sheep – Billy, Goat and Gruff – into a box, which she passed to a man to give to a new kid. The man then took Woody's friend out to his car.

As the man went back inside the house, Woody hurried down to
see Bo. "Quick!" he cried. "We'll sneak in the hedges."

But Bo knew she couldn't go back. "It's time for the next kid," she said.

She wanted Woody to come with her, but the cowboy couldn't leave Andy.
They both said goodbye and Woody watched his friend leave, knowing he
might never see her again.

Many years later, Woody and the gang belonged to a young girl called Bonnie. On her induction day at preschool, Woody wanted to make sure she was okay, so he hid himself in her bag and went with her.

At preschool, Bonnie made a toy out of a plastic spork and other bits and pieces – she called it Forky.

Woody felt good seeing Bonnie so happy, but was very surprised when Forky's eyes moved. The spork was alive!

Back in Bonnie's room, Woody told the toys that Bonnie had made a new friend at preschool. "Everyone, I want you to meet… Forky!"

They were just as surprised as Woody had been. Forky, however, was very confused. He didn't understand how important he was to Bonnie and believed he was a piece of rubbish.

Woody had to spend the rest of the night stopping Forky from throwing himself in the bin.

A few days later, Bonnie and her family went on a road trip. She'd taken all her toys with her, including Forky. The spork was still desperate to escape and, one night, while Bonnie was sleeping, he jumped out of a window.

Woody knew he had to go after him, so he climbed up to the window and said to the other toys, "I'll meet you at the RV park." Woody then jumped out of the campervan, too.

Woody called out for Forky. He soon found the spork by the side of the road and began dragging him towards the RV park. On the way, Woody tried to get Forky to realise how important he was to Bonnie. He explained that she loved Forky the same way Forky loved rubbish.

Forky finally understood what Woody meant. "She must be feeling awful without me," the spork said, breaking into a run. "We've got to get going, she needs me!"

Soon after, they came to a town called Grand Basin. Nearby there was a carnival and the RV park.

Both Woody and Forky would soon be with Bonnie again!

Making his way down the dark street, Woody's eyes fixed upon a lamp shining in the window of an antique shop. It was the lamp that belonged to his friend, Bo. Was she in there? Woody was worried she had become a lost toy.

Woody had to know if Bo was in the antique shop, so he went inside with Forky. The pair soon bumped into a dummy called Benson and a doll named Gabby Gabby.

Woody tried to leave with Forky, but the doll wouldn't let them. Gabby Gabby wanted Woody's voicebox to replace her broken one.

She believed this was why no child wanted her. Woody escaped when the antique shop owner's granddaughter, Harmony, found him on the floor and took him to a playground in a park.

Forky wasn't so lucky. Gabby Gabby and her dummies had captured him inside the antique shop.

At the park, Woody frantically searched for a way to get back to the antique shop and rescue Forky. Sneaking across the playground, Woody saw a group of toys waiting excitedly to be played with.

Suddenly, a large group of children turned up and, as they played with all the toys, Woody came face-to-face with an old friend.

It was Bo Peep! Woody learnt how Bo was now a lost toy, but that she'd been having lots of adventures, including helping other lost toys get played with. Bo also introduced the cowboy to one of her new friends, Officer Giggle McDimples.

Billy, Goat and Gruff were happy to see Woody, too!

Woody said he needed help to rescue Forky from Gabby Gabby and bring him back to Bonnie. Bo and Giggle were reluctant at first, as they didn't want to go back to the antique shop, but Woody was able to convince them to help.

Meanwhile, Buzz had left the RV park to go looking for Woody. Unfortunately, he'd been found by a carnival worker and was now the top prize in the Star Adventurer game! This upset two attached toys called Ducky and Bunny, whose place as top prize had been taken by Buzz.

With Bunny's help, Ducky started kicking Buzz, causing all three toys to fall to the ground. Now he was free, the space ranger quickly resumed his search for Woody. Ducky and Bunny chased after him as they felt Buzz owed them a kid.

It didn't take long for Buzz, Ducky and Bunny to find Woody,
along with Bo, the sheep and Giggle McDimples on the roof of the
antique shop. Woody explained what happened and that they were on
their way to rescue Forky.

So, with Bo leading the way down the shaft, the group entered the
antique shop.

Once inside, Bo pointed out Gabby Gabby's glass cabinet. It was the
most likely place to find Forky. It would be very risky to get to, but Bo
had a plan.

Desperate to rescue Forky, Woody didn't stick to the plan and ran towards the cabinet, only to find it was locked. Bo yanked Woody to the ground. She was frustrated that he didn't follow her plan.

Then, a dummy grabbed Woody! To protect their friend, Bo's sheep bit on to the dummy's trousers, but the dummy ran off – with the sheep still attached to him.

Bo was annoyed at Woody for not following the plan, but she was determined to get her sheep back. She sprinted further into the antique shop, as Woody followed behind.

Bo took Woody to meet her friend, Duke Caboom, Canada's greatest stuntman. Bo told him Gabby Gabby had Forky and her sheep and that she needed him to jump onto a cabinet.

Duke had no confidence and refused to do the jump. But with Bo's encouragement, Duke felt his confidence return and agreed to help.

With everything ready, it was time to rescue Forky and Bo's sheep.

With their plan put into action, Bo was soon reunited with her sheep, but they accidentally woke up Dragon – a cat who lived in the shop. Duke helped Woody and the others escape, but they hadn't rescued the spork. "Forky's still in there," said Woody. "If we hurry, we can get him before they lock him up."

But none of the toys were in any sort of shape to try and rescue Forky again. They left for the carnival, leaving Woody to go back into the shop alone.

Woody entered the shop just as it was about to close. "Hello, Woody," said Gabby Gabby. "I knew you'd be back."

Woody thought he'd have to fight to get Forky. But Gabby Gabby only wanted Woody to understand her. "I was defective right out of the box," she continued. All she wanted was the chance to be important to a kid. "I'd give anything to be loved the way you have."

Woody agreed to give Gabby Gabby his voicebox. "Just leave me Forky. Bonnie needs him."

Even with a voicebox, Harmony thought Gabby Gabby was too creepy. Seeing this, Woody decided he'd take the doll to Bonnie. Having returned to the shop, the other toys agreed to help.

As they headed back to Bonnie, Gabby Gabby saw a lost girl crying. The other toys made sure the girl noticed Gabby Gabby sitting nearby.

"Are you lost, too?" the girl asked, picking up the doll. "I'll help you."

The girl hugged Gabby Gabby tight and went to ask a security guard for help. The doll had finally found a child who loved her for who she was.

Woody and Bo met up with Bonnie's toys at the campervan and everyone was happy to see them. Woody was even happier to see Bonnie reunited with Forky. Woody had done the job he'd set out to do.

It was then he realised that there were kids and toys everywhere who would always need his help. He loved seeing kids playing with toys and toys finding happiness with kids.

Woody knew that wherever he went and whichever toy he helped next, he would always have his friends by his side.